For all the dreamers of the world.
And for you, Mom. —B.L.

Text and illustrations copyright © 2016 by Becky Laff

KAR-BEN PUBLISHING
A division of Lerner Publishing Group, Inc.
241 First Avenue North
Minneapolis, MN 55401 USA
1-800-4-KARBEN

Website address: www.karben.com

Main body text set in CCDaveGibbonsLower regular.

Library of Congress Cataloging-in-Publication Data

Names: Laff, Becky, author.
Title: Joseph the dreamer / by Becky Laff.
Description: Minneapolis, MN : Kar-Ben Publishing, a division of
    Lerner Publishing Group, [2016] | 2016
Identifiers: LCCN 2015040987 (print) | LCCN 2015041240 (ebook)
    | ISBN 9781467778459 (lb : alk. paper) | ISBN 9781467778503
    (pb : alk. paper) | ISBN 9781512409352 (eb pdf)
Subjects: LCSH: Joseph (Son of Jacob)–Juvenile literature. |
    Brothers–Juvenile literature. | Jealousy–Juvenile literature. | Bible
    stories, English–Genesis.
Classification: LCC BS580.J6 L24 2016 (print) |
    LCC BS580.J6 (ebook) | DDC 222/.11092–dc23

LC record available at http://lccn.loc.gov/2015040987

Manufactured in the United States of America
1 – PC – 7/15/16

JOSEPH
THE DREAMER

Adapted from Genesis

words and art by **Becky Laff**

KAR-BEN
PUBLISHING

Let me tell you the story of Joseph.

It all began many, many years ago— *thousands* of years ago.

Joseph lived in the Land of Canaan, where he grew up in a very large family.

People far and wide knew of his father, Jacob, who was a good man.

Jacob's lands stretched for miles. He had fields of corn and wheat and many grasslands for grazing his herds of sheep.

Joseph's early life was like a dream.

As the 11th of 12 sons, Joseph would not inherit any of Jacob's lands.

But Jacob made sure to let him and everyone else know that Joseph was first in his heart.

8

10

One warm, sunny day...

Joseph's brothers led him to the farthest reaches of their family's lands.

This way, Joseph. A bit of fence needs mending...

But then...

Now what?

Should we just leave him here in this pit?

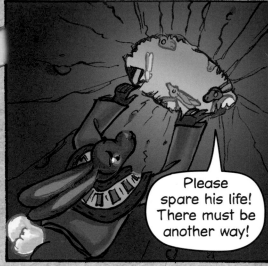

Please spare his life! There must be another way!

Look! There's a group of Ishmaelite tradesmen!

What if we SOLD Joseph to them as a slave?

Hmmmm. Then Joseph's fate would be left for God to decide...

...and we would not be to blame!

A deal was struck....

Joseph's brothers sold him into slavery.

And Joseph was taken away from everything he had known and loved.

What was to become of Joseph now?

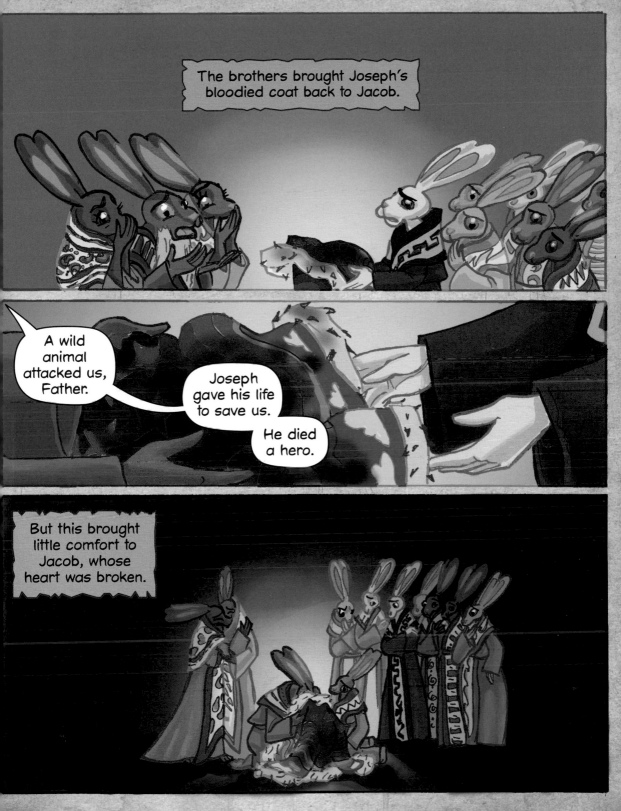

20

The Ishmaelites had sold him to a wealthy and powerful merchant called Potiphar.

Potiphar's estate was far grander than anything Joseph had seen before. Joseph was eager to learn about this new world.

Oh, I've dropped my handkerchief!

Here, I'll get it, my lady...

JOSEPH!!!!

How DARE you kiss my wife?!

Oh, my husband! You came just in time!

GRRRRRRRRR

But I did nothing wrong!

ENOUGH! I'll have you thrown in jail for this!

GUARDS! Take him out of my sight!

So again, Joseph was taken away.

And now Joseph feared he would never see the light of day again.

It wasn't long before the guards also came to Joseph for advice.

They could see he was special, and they gave him gifts of extra food and conversation.

Those kind words meant so much to Joseph, because most of the time...

...he was very much alone.

In his loneliness, he saw only darkness around him.

Sometimes it felt as if it was pressing on him, *crushing* him.

The days seemed to blend together.

29

One day, two men were put into Joseph's cell.

I'm Pharaoh's baker.

I'm Pharaoh's butler.

Neither knew if they would live or die.

And both had been having vivid dreams.

Tell me of these dreams which haunt you and I will tell you their meaning.

In the butler's dream, he was picking grapes from the Pharaoh's garden.

He crushed them into a fine, fragrant wine.

Then he served this wine to Pharaoh, who drank deeply from the cup.

This is a good dream!

Whatever upset Pharaoh will pass. He will soon release you and restore you to your position.

I hope I am wrong about this!

But as the days wore on, Joseph's predictions proved to be true.

I'm free! I'm going back to Pharaoh's palace. I'll tell Pharaoh of your plight. He'll release you!

But Joseph would remain in the darkness of his prison cell for another 2 years...

The butler must have forgotten his promise.

But then something *miraculous* began to happen.

Haunting dreams began to disturb Egypt's pharaoh.

And now Pharaoh's butler remembered his long forgotten promise.

AAAAAAHHHHHH!!!!!!

In prison I met a man called Joseph. He interprets dreams!

Then let him be brought before me!

34

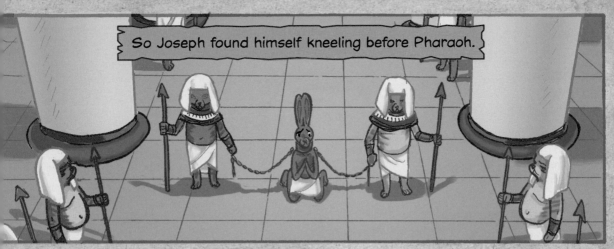

So Joseph found himself kneeling before Pharaoh.

He was frightened but he had faith in himself.

Tell me of these dreams which haunt you, O Great One, and I will tell you their meaning.

And Pharaoh sat with Joseph and told him of his visions.

Hmmmm...

...hmmm...

AHA!

Egypt will have seven years in a row of bountiful harvests—but that will be followed by seven years of drought and famine....

Of course, that would take a lot of planning...

Pharaoh could prepare for that by storing the extra grain during the good years...?

I'm sure Mighty Pharaoh already has a solution in mind.

And then Pharaoh could see what everyone else had always seen...

Joseph had reached the height of success.

He was popular as well as powerful.

But he was still hurt by what had happened in his past.

The brothers were starving and ate eagerly.

Meanwhile, Joseph set his trap right under their noses.

They didn't see him slip a golden cup into Benjamin's bag.

At last, when the feast was over and the brothers were full...

One of my precious golden cups is MISSING!

Someone has stolen it!

GUARDS!

Search these Canaanites' bags!

So at last, all was forgiven!

Soon, Jacob came to Egypt.

And with him, he brought Joseph's beautiful, rainbow-colored coat!

A coat fit for a KING!

Joseph!

My dearest son, I've prayed for this day to come for so long.

How proud I am of you!

I've missed you so much, Father! How I've longed for my family.

And now Joseph could feel happiness fill his heart with light...